Abigale
the Happy Whale

Peter Farrelly illustrated by **Jamie Rama**

 Megan Tingley Books
LITTLE, BROWN AND COMPANY
New York ❧ Boston

For Bob and Apple
—P.F.

For my little creatures Ellie and Sullivan
—J.R.

Text copyright © 2006 by Peter Farrelly   Illustrations copyright © 2006 by Jamie Rama

Little, Brown and Company   •   Time Warner Book Group   •   1271 Avenue of the Americas, New York, NY 10020   •   Visit our Web site at www.lb-kids.com

First Edition: June 2006

Library of Congress Cataloging-in-Publication Data

Farrelly, Peter.

Abigale the happy whale / by Peter Farrelly : illustrated by Jamie Rama.—1st ed.

p. cm.

Summary: Abigale comes up with a "whale" of an idea to prevent Land People from polluting the sea.

ISBN 0-316-01190-8

[1. Marine pollution—Fiction. 2. Pollution—Fiction. 3. Humpback whale—Fiction. 4. Whales—Fiction. 5. Marine animals—Fiction.] I. Rama, Jamie, ill. II. Title.

PZ7. F24613Abi 2006

[E]—dc22   2005005734

10 9 8 7 6 5 4 3 2 1

SC

Manufactured in China

The text was set in Cushing, and the display type is Jimbo.

Once upon a time, a large family of humpback whales swam through the Santa Monica Bay toward the beaches of California. The sight of humpbacks was common in these waters — but these humpbacks were different. They were very quiet, and very, very sad. They paddled along, never looking back or singing or smiling. And strangest of all, these whales hardly even bothered to eat.

Except for Abigale the Happy Whale. She swam at the very back of the group, like the caboose of a train, which was about how big she was. As she floated past the coolers and refrigerators and broken glass that litterbugs had dumped on the ocean floor, Abigale ate about as much as a little whale can eat.

When she wasn't singing or laughing or eating, Abigale was playing with her friends, the smaller Sea People.

For a while the Golfin' Dolphin putted alongside her. Boy, was he ever teed off. One of the Land People had thrown a golf club into the sea and clobbered him on the snout. Abigale gave him a big kiss. This made him feel better.

"Do you have time to play eighteen holes?" the Golfin' Dolphin asked.

"I can't today," she said. "We're on our way to the beach."

"To the beach?" the confused dolphin repeated. "How can a whale go to the beach?"

He didn't get an answer, though, for Abigale was gone.

The whales continued to swim over junked cars and shipwrecks and lost Frisbees, and Abigale didn't stop until she ran into her old friend Clem the Clam. Clem was acting like a real dip because someone had dropped an old television set on his clam bed.

"What kind of chowderhead would do something like this?" the steamed clam snapped.

Abigale the Happy Whale couldn't answer, but because she dug this shellfish, she pushed the television off his clam bed.

"I've got to go now," she said. "We're on our way to the beach."

Clem was so surprised he clammed up.

The whales swam over rusty anchors and fishing poles covered with green gunk, and even a mirror framed in barnacles. That's where Abigale saw Blackie the Goldfish and Fred Doofish the Red Bluefish.

"How are you guys?" Abigale asked.

"Terrible!" Blackie the Goldfish cried. "I've got more oil on me than a can of sardines."

"Well, at least your problems are only scale-deep," Fred Doofish the Red Bluefish said. "I've got a liver the size of a beanbag chair, and I'm turning red from the inside out."

This was because Fred had eaten seaweed that was polluted by a nearby factory.

"I don't care what you look like or how big your livers are," Abigale said. "I still love you both."

Fred and Blackie smiled and watched the Happy Whale splash
away past an empty cat food can and a broken beach chair.

"Where are you going, Abigale?" they called out.

"To the beach," she said, and their mouths dropped open like
a couple of surprised fish, which is what they were.

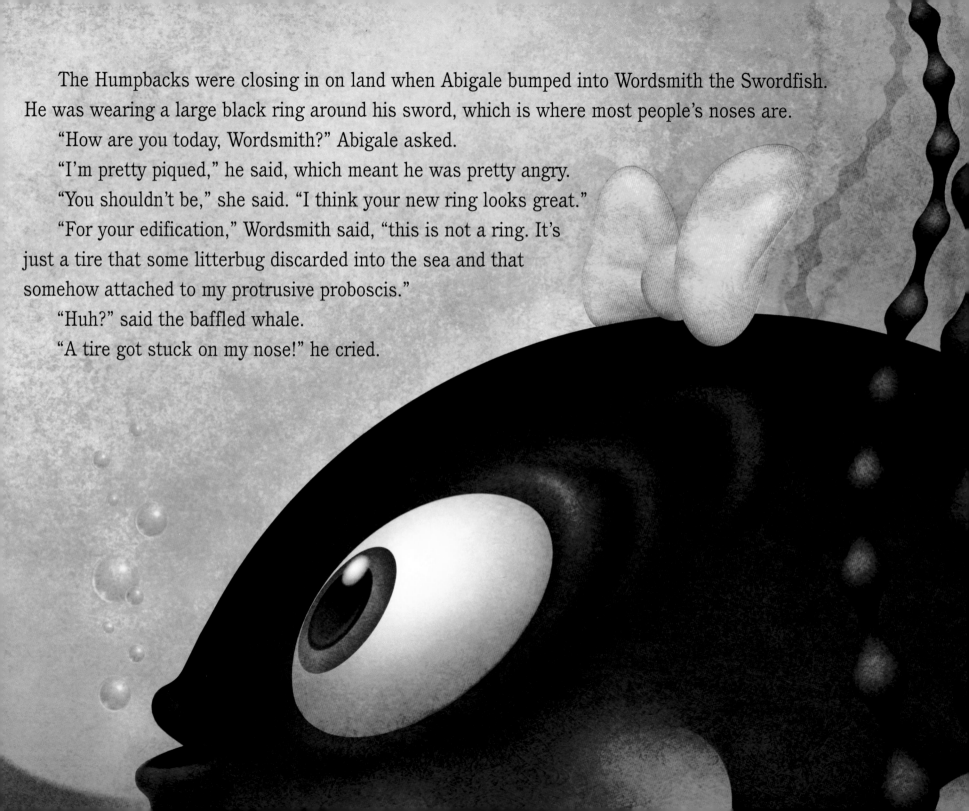

The Humpbacks were closing in on land when Abigale bumped into Wordsmith the Swordfish. He was wearing a large black ring around his sword, which is where most people's noses are.

"How are you today, Wordsmith?" Abigale asked.

"I'm pretty piqued," he said, which meant he was pretty angry.

"You shouldn't be," she said. "I think your new ring looks great."

"For your edification," Wordsmith said, "this is not a ring. It's just a tire that some litterbug discarded into the sea and that somehow attached to my protrusive proboscis."

"Huh?" said the baffled whale.

"A tire got stuck on my nose!" he cried.

Luckily, Abigale was able to talk Dr. Gus the Octopus into making a house call. After the good doctor had jacked Wordsmith up and had pulled the whitewall off the swordfish's snout, he asked Abigale where she was off to.

"We're going to the beach," she said, and she started to drift away.

Well, let me tell you, Dr. Gus the Octopus was up in arms over this. Using his good seven arms (the doctor had hurt his eighth arm on a pop-top from a soda can), he ran and caught Abigale.

"Whales can't go to the beach!" Dr. Gus insisted. "You'll all get stuck in the sand."

Abigale frowned. "Why would we be going to the beach if it would hurt us?" she wondered aloud.

Abigale the Happy Whale swam past all the sad, quiet whales until she got to the Head Whale, Ed Dale.
"Why are we going to the beach?" she asked him. "Dr. Gus the Octopus said it could be dangerous."
"We're not going to the beach," said Ed Dale the Head Whale. "We're beaching ourselves."
"But then we'll get stuck in the sand," Abigale said.

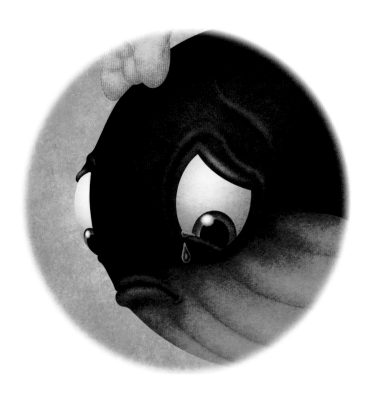

A tear rolled out of her eye.

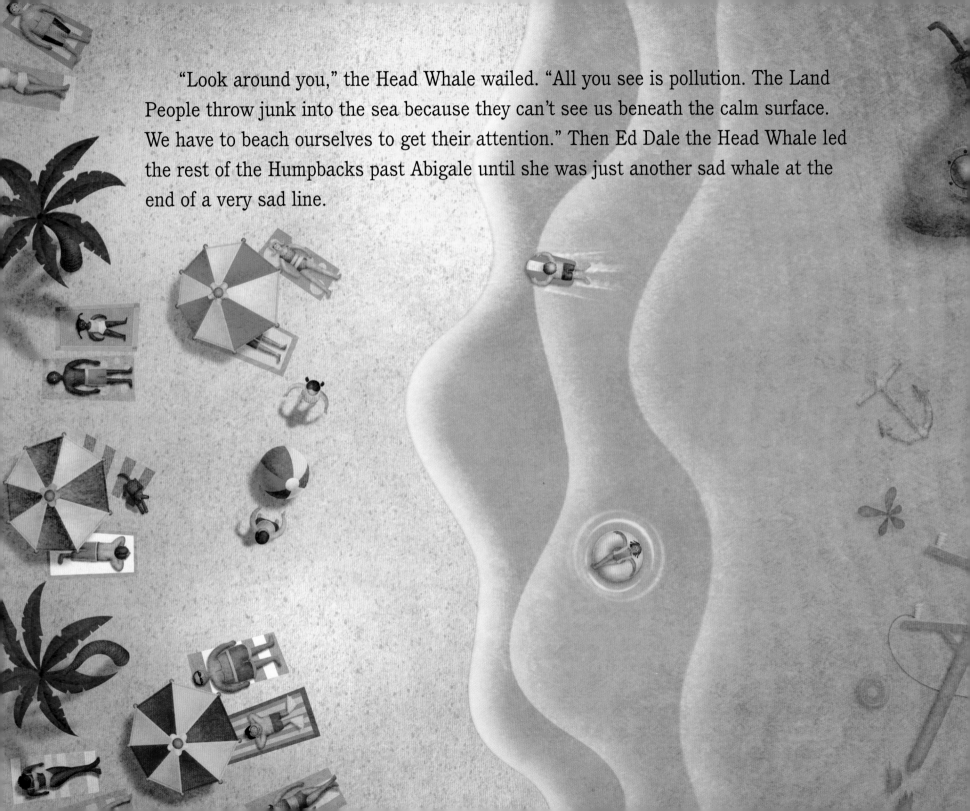

"Look around you," the Head Whale wailed. "All you see is pollution. The Land People throw junk into the sea because they can't see us beneath the calm surface. We have to beach ourselves to get their attention." Then Ed Dale the Head Whale led the rest of the Humpbacks past Abigale until she was just another sad whale at the end of a very sad line.

The family of Humpbacks was only a few hundred yards from shore when Abigale passed under the broad shadow of Moby Duck. Moby was the biggest duck in the world because oil had spilled from a ship onto his feathers. At first he looked like a licorice duck, but then things started sticking to him. Pretty soon he looked like a floating junkyard.

This is what stuck to Moby Duck:

Two buoys with blinking lights

A plastic bat

Three Styrofoam cups

Seven life preservers

**Four bottles with messages in them
(Two without)**

A doll with one arm

A sofa

A hamburger container

Twenty-two corks

A small rowboat

A clogged-up snorkel

A large rowboat

**And a pair of men's size 48 underwear that had the words BE MY VALENTiNE
written on them in red**

Needless to say, Moby Duck was feeling down.

"What are you doing so close to the shore?" Moby quacked.

"We're beaching ourselves," Abigale whispered in a choked-up voice.

"Oh, no!" the sad duck cried. "Why would you do something like that?"

"We have to let the Land People see us, so they'll stop polluting," the young whale replied.

"But that won't accomplish anything," Moby Duck said. "After all, they see me and they still pollute."

Abigale realized that this duck covered with yuck had a point. Beaching themselves wouldn't help anybody; it would only add to the litter.

That's when she decided to take matters into her own fins.

Abigale skimmed across the ocean floor and in one big gulp ate a soup can, a tennis racquet, a compass, and a boot. Then she came to the surface and blew the stuff right out of the spout on her back and onto the beach. The other Sea People had had it up to their gills with pollution too, so they joined in to lend a helping fin.

The Golfin' Dolphin chipped in by whacking an old volleyball onto the beach with a golf club.

Dr. Gus the Octopus tossed a six-pack of soda bottles and a rusty Thermos at the same time.

Wordsmith the Swordfish carved up an old ladder for Blackie the Goldfish and Fred Doofish the Red Bluefish to carry piece by piece to the shore.

Clem the Clam was always willing to stick out his neck for friends, so he helped out too. Before long, all of the Sea People were cleaning up the water.

The Dogfish, Rin Fin Fin, was barking out orders to Sid the Squid and Neil the Eel.

Tab the Crab was there in a pinch, and Bob the Lobster turned out to be an unselfish shellfish.

Shucks, folks, even Rose Royster the Rich Oyster went to work for a while.

When Ed Dale the Head Whale saw what was happening, he too began gobbling up the garbage and blowing it back onto the shore through his great spout.

Soon all the other whales started doing the same. In a little less than one afternoon, they swept the entire sea clean. And they had a whale of a time!

When the Land People saw all their junk coming back at them, they had no choice but to clean it up and properly dispose of it. After all, if they didn't, there wouldn't be room to go to the beach. Big trucks came from far away and hauled everything off to the real junkyards. The junk that went on the final truck was the stuff they pulled off Moby Duck.

Then the school of whales swam back out to sea.
And for the first time in a long time, they were all as
happy as Abigale the Happy Whale!